DOMESTICATION
HANDBOOK

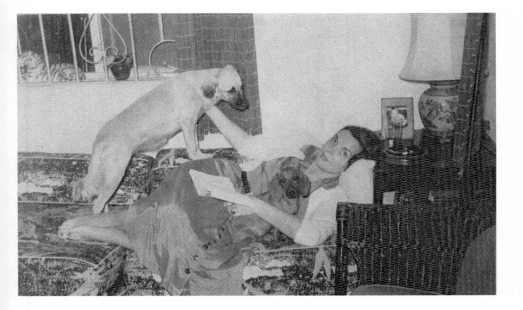

DOMESTICATION
HANDBOOK

KRISTEN STONE

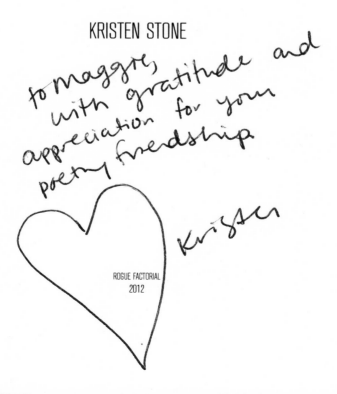

*to maggie,
with gratitude and
appreciation for your
poetry friendship*

kristen

ROGUE FACTORIAL
2012

For my mother, who loves the little animals
and Luthien, the newest one.

Contents

Before

Once, I was a swimming comma, spine curved like a mineral taproot. Waiting for the mirror stage when I could think without words, *mine*. The pause between ideas, the caught breath while reading.

Before learning to ride a bike (my mother, pregnant with my youngest sister, running up and down the gutter of the quiet street; she gripped the seat of the gray bicycle; I yelped and flew, afraid). Before the exchange of candy for reading: a sugar-fueled move towards literacy. Round chocolates in a kindergarten classroom for connecting shapes on cards to sounds: the curved lines glittered and took form.

The moment of recognition: the first time I saw Queen Anne's lace and knew that I did not belong anywhere, for going elsewhere and knowing the names of things I'd never seen before.

The moment my mother knew I was a baby in there. A person beginning outside language, these things happen: she slept next to my father but I was closer (within).

Then: a nest where the little mammals go to bury their facts

Digging with hooked paws. Soft pads walk only on soil, never pavement. (Like the puppy's pink feet, before his first walk, a proud time. They with a new dog, a gleaming bear.) (A bad dog who didn't listen. The father shouted and pulled the leash. The dog fell down; they flushed, embarrassed, sick.) (Pride in a new thing never lasted long. Not for faith though it seemed just for meanness. At least if it was a religious lesson they could hate God in secret.)

In the closet there is a pile of dresses from the thrift store. Bonnets, for playing prairie. A dress like a Sunday school teacher might wear. The high-heeled shoes had glitter and were royal blue. The mother wore them once to an insurance banquet, at a hotel. (They and all the other children in their pajamas watched Disney movies with a hotel babysitter. They refused to go to sleep with strangers, waited up stubborn for their shining parents to return.)

Sometimes when they played Emergency Room they had to hide the children afterwards. The red nail polish would not rub off their plastic limbs. Only spoiled children, or animals, destroyed things on purpose. Smothered under dresses that smelled like strangers' skin.

Once they forgot a Barbie in the swimming pool and her rubber legs bleached white. That was funny. Everyone thought so.

A baby with a heart problem was left on the doorstep. An orphan. Orphans were sad, but not unbearably so. They were allowed. The little mammals laid her out on the blue bookshelf. They pricked a needle into her jointless plastic arm. Got her some fluids—a Ziploc bag IV.

Oh no. She needs a blood transfusion. One squeezes the food coloring into the bag. She is careful but it gets on her hands. The dye bleeds into all her cracks. Watching it is like water drying on the pavement when a storm ends.

With the X-Acto knife she splits the beanbag chest. Plastic pills inside, for organs and muscles. She digs them away, places the sewing machine pedal there. *Nurse,* she says sternly. The other little mammal is there then. They sew her up. The importance tingles on their hands like germs.

They bandage her chest tight; the machine hums. Life support.

PART I

A BASIC GUIDE

TO FARMING

It is dangerous to care about something which cannot love you back like plants and certain animals.

It is dangerous to worry over an embryonic plant in a hard round coat which we press into the soil knowing it feeds us.

At the Allegan County Fair

1.

The rhesus monkey paces in its cage. The man in the safari suit stands with a brutal posture, hips thrown forward. To conquer. He wanted to be a lion tamer, but lions are too expensive. He makes do with a cage full of lemurs, two parrots, a small fox, and a pair of porcupines.

They travel on the interstate in a trailer with glass walls. They can see traffic go by. The same way cows can, on their way to the slaughterhouse. When they stick their noses out at you. Big wet noses, round, like a mushroom.

2.

To get into the fairgrounds we walk between a wall of Pioneer Corn and the Child Evangelism Mission. Even though it's illegal, sometimes corn volunteers in a field of soybeans. The stalk or two standing tall like the lone Tea Party patriot on a street corner, with his flag. *Don't tread on me.*

This is corn country—corn and soybeans. We'll see soybeans in the exhibition barn, resting on Styrofoam trays. *The best of our county's bountiful agriculture.*

A cheerful woman asks Hazel if she wants to see a magic trick. Hazel grimaces. *I guess not*, the missionary says, kind of rude, and turns her back to us.

Take My Hand, Not My Life, implores an enormous baby on a vinyl poster.

Embedded in the ashy soil like a stubborn embryo.

3.

Mari insists we go on the Ferris wheel. The sensation familiar like a dream: the sweep and fall a sick thrill. The view is unimpressive: food vendors with their greasy stuff; the smaller rides crammed with people determined to enjoy themselves. We fly down and around again, the sky clearing as the sun goes down. Over the muddy fair and in the bandshell: "Sweet Home Alabama," though this is Michigan. The animals engorged and sleepy: the prize bull lying on his side like a black, furred elephant, and the chickens who hide their faces.

As we fly around again we note that the rides need to be taken apart and packed up and put back together somewhere new.

Investment mission

I wake in corn country to *hundreds of millions of potential consumers*. I wake next to the neighbor's soybeans, to *a booming middle class*. I wake to your breast in my hand and I try to be tender, our priorities are clear.

Tell them to reconsider. Tell them, *go back to bed*.

I drive home: the *global economy* in the front seat with the sleeping dog. *Mutually assured destruction only makes sense to sane, rational people. Tribes* who live in *caves* don't care about the *global economy*: our priorities are clear. I drive home with *Maoist insurgents. They claim to be acting on behalf of the poor and indigenous*, a leading academic who studies the *Maoist insurgents* says.

Won't listen till you ask nice. Is that any way to get what you want?

(Our priorities are clear.)

Safety is a shared responsibility, the governor of West Virginia tells me. *Miners who die in these tragic accidents don't die in vain: we pass new safety legislation.*

(Whose jungle?)
(Whose mountain?)
(Whose cave?)

At dawn I am not just a warm body waking: it is mine explosions on the radio and also the chirping phone—

It is the dog in a crate downstairs, his fur wild behind the straight black lines. *Crate* is a nice word for *cage* although experts recommend it: the crate functions as a wolf's den would, in the wild, to make the dog feel safe.

It is a barn full of goats; two pigs fat and waiting.
Who can fill the hole under the ocean? Say the serenity prayer.
Governor's gone to Russia. Let's go back to sleep.

A creek runs between the neighbor's apples (sprayed yesterday) and the next neighbor's soybeans. A ditch, for runoff. What is pushed to the edges. Some things I can name: autumn olive, wild strawberries, Queen Anne's lace, milkweed. Others I can't, so they blend together.

Shorthand

The smell of leeks reminds me of the Netherlands in November
the three weeks I spent there with a traveling band of American feminists

We drank espresso and sat smoking in the hostel lobby
so cold always and the leaves a bright red against old brick.

I wore a borrowed coat and we all had nervous breakdowns
I was colder than I had words for, my thin Southern blood running fast.

We read Deleuze in a cement lecture hall and the sky felt too close
the church bells rang anarchy, whenever they felt like it.

We ate leek soup, and chocolate bars in purple paper with a cow on the front.
Extra Romig—I still don't know what that means.

And I slept in Marina's bed every night, partly because I was cold
but also because I wanted to be in love with someone, so far from home.

I had to feed strange, ugly coins into a public phone in the middle of the night to
   call my mother
my voice traveling over six hours and an ocean, a distance that requires abstraction:
we talked to each other on two different days.

One night I was lonely and trying to wake Marina up to hold me closer (or touch
   my hipbone)
and still asleep she kissed the back of my neck. The thrill lasted for over an hour.

We should have met at fourteen rather than twenty, we could have been in love then.
Wrinkled hands, tattoos under her tights—if I couldn't be warm I wanted poetry.

Anatomy Lessons

1.

If a pepper touches the ground as it grows
its poor bottom will get black and soft
useless for keeping inside and outside apart.

Sad rotten bottoms, Gregory and I sing
as we prepare for the frost,
picking peppers before they're red.

2.

Children's pigs at the fair are unashamed of their naked, human bottoms.
Potbellied 4H dads guide the pigs with sheets of plywood.
One panics in the arena: a confused pink monster.

3.

The intrinsic sense that the bottom should be kept towards the wall,
something strange could happen to it:
the soft round butter pat could just fly away.

One day your father will tell you all the terrible things:
maybe they happened to you too.

Sav-a-kid

1.

When a kid is about to die, there is a moment when the straw itches your legs
the heat lamp burns and the horror fades:
Should we try the bottle one more time?
No, maybe not.

This is the death you mourn
although six others died from the same infection
plus Charlotte with two more curled inside her.
(She's composting behind the barn, now, in rotting straw.)

2.

Returning to pre-mammalian stem cells, he evolves in reverse:
A chimpanzee, then a deer, trilobite posture,
finally just Cambrian hard parts:
the skeleton to store minerals needed for life
blurred lines, fur matted like a map
with shit and piss and the things we try to feed him:
Gatorade, milk, the empty promise of name-brand formula

He went away, you keep saying,
after the shuddering moment when his eyes roll back
he stiffens then a gurgle and then, extinguished.
Simple forces take over: a thing bent out of shape
by its temporary inhabitant,
limbs drift back to neutral.

A little more air moves but you keep saying, *he went away—*

3.

You tell Tom *we just lost him* and he doesn't hear.
Everything the same? he asks
and you have to repeat yourself.

*No matter how many animals you have
a loss is still a loss*, he says
which sounds economic
although I think he is trying to be tender.

4.

You lie on the couch, the dog curls on your back
your face smells of milk shit: yeasty and sweet.

Is it safe to live this close to death?
This proximity will distort your features
make you hear things in the night
and feel a pulse in organs others lack.

The thing with feathers

Deb asks have I seen the injured chicken. I do not know what she means so I follow her into the tool shed. She opens a wonderland door I never knew was there. A chicken is there, a round brown bird that does not move.

Deb picks her up. Shows me her dead foot, one wing like a heavy fist. She sets her down by the bruised tomato she's brought. *I keep her in here because she gets hurt if she's with the other chickens. Everyone forgets she's here, but I try and remember to feed her and now you can too.*

Deb, once a rancher's daughter, now a farmer's wife, saves this one chicken as she eats others. Hides it from Richard's culling hands. So Victorian, the invalid hidden, the secret initiation of the attic infirmary or the hidden coop. The beautiful obligation of caring for something that can give you nothing in return.

Why haven't they killed it, asks Jasmine later. (What she means is, *you should eat this one.*)

The injured chicken falls from good foot to lame one, weighted by her dead wing in her little straw room with a cracked window.

Why Wilbur when Fern eats bacon? Why the injured chicken sustained? *Some animals are pets and some are food*, Deb's little girl tells me: she doesn't eat animals she knows.

When you see the axe or a broken wing you feel the rupture.
The shift in the breastbone that means you're in love.

The animal question

(The perfect butch lover is steady and practical. She is not like blood or air. Taut muscled forearms and a warm towel, she is *helpful*. She will kneel in the straw for as long as it takes.)

Yesterday she delivered baby goats. One kid had its leg tucked up alongside its body. They are supposed to dive out, though: the long journey from liquid to air. The amniotic sac bulged. Then there was fluid. A glistening alien puddle wetted the straw.

The glove went up to her elbow. She reached inside to move the leg. Tom, his ears covered with a blue fleece headband, coached. *Which side is it on?* He asked. *Can you feel the nose?*

Let me try again, okay, sweetheart, she murmured, intent. (It was like the night before.) I clenched and throbbed in mammal empathy. Noises almost familiar.

An education in electricity and green things

1.

Cathy is holding a kid between her knees. Its head is trapped in a special box. She is holding a hot thing which is buzzing. She is pressing it into the goat's head. It is making a sound. It is screaming.

(The goat book reassures: it's quick, humane, and painless. The goat could tear an eye out. Disbudding protects them from nature. Just playing is dangerous, with horns. And how would you build a hay manger or a stanchion for such beastly livestock?)

Cathy presses the tip at an angle into the raw head meat. *I'm sorry, sweetheart.* The barn is full of smoke. It smells like diesel and gunpowder and singed hair.

2.

They go outside for the first time. They are three weeks old. The world brightened and grew. The world is contained by white mesh, which holds a spark harnessed by a small solar panel on the side of the barn.

Cathy says, *yes children, touch it with your nose.* They jump back. They cluster in the soft green middle. There are ugly red holes in their heads, where the horns would have grown. The hair is singed around the craters, which reach down to their skulls. They don't know that they look tortured.

We teach them to drink water, holding our wet hands to their soft mouths. They suckle. (A soft ache in my nipples.) We carry them out under our arms. Two at a time they scramble.

Learn sunlight. Rumen. Learn grass. Learn to go back into the barn the same way you came out.

The Miracle of Life at the Chelsea Community Fair

Here we learn about being born:
an incubator of eggs we can watch until they crack.
The cow waits, chained, for her time.

Please do not touch the cow.
Please touch the corn and soybean display.

We can watch veterinary students
spay a dog behind a heavy canvas tarp:
the screen overhead to show the pulsing and stitches
claustrophobic space inside her body wet blue.

A model of a cow offers rubber teats you can squeeze *the old fashioned way.*

The United Dairy Industry of Michigan
gives me a coloring book:
a cow with earrings and a fat happy bell
tells how milk is processed.

A special truck comes to the farm. The milk from the tank is piped into the truck.
The truck drives my milk to the dairy plant.
Milk is in the milk group. Milk helps build _____.

The correct answer is "healthy bones and teeth."
Thank Goodness for Cows.
Are you now or have you ever been
a radical environmentalist? A vegan?

Sperm from the bull is inserted into the female cow's cervix
which is how cows are impregnated on many farms.
Someone who didn't already know the role of bodies in reproduction
would leave wondering if all births were artificial.

(*Transparency* means thick plastic. The incubator and its hot gold light, like a yolk.)

Dual purpose

In Mary's animal science class they broke open twenty-one eggs, each a day older than the one before. By day three, a tiny heart. *Hours matter,* said the matter-of-fact professor, telling students to check their impulse to save the last chick. *It won't make it.*

At market Jack says, *when we were kids it was all organic.* He and Victoria scream at each other because neither can hear. Full of love they shuffle from their truck to their card table and back, shouting anecdotes. He used to be Buzz Aldrin's dentist: a filling he made went to space.

Jack tells me the duck eggs are fertile. He has a feather in his cap and I believe him. I was only looking for something to take to my sweetheart, for dinner, something for her to cook in the dim Lansing kitchen. But he said I could hatch them. He's been a poultry guy since World War II so he knows.

I slipped eight under a chicken. *9/18 duck egg don't eat,* gently penciled on each shell. Those to try and become animals. Four she scrambled. Two each on plates, next to toast.

An eggshell is tough and thick and faintly striped. At the Miracle of Life I learned that a dome is best: it distributes force evenly and does not break. My mother used to say *walking on eggshells* but this is not what she meant.

There is nothing to do but wait and see, for twenty-eight days. Today, day twenty, they can hear.

(Inside: all the knowledge to become a baby bird. Proteins and amino acid chains. A golden web clings to mineral walls. All the strongest shapes.)

Lessons in proportion

What happens is the fingertips crack. Massage them with salve, holy like a leper's feet: a fox creeps in, licks it all off in the night. Hands smell like dead meat and rosemary in the morning.

Threaten to fold and break apart like an overloved paper doll. Laura Ingalls, flat, without a head.

Play with paper dolls in the corner while you worry about being murdered. Stand the fold-up scene against the wall. Perform *Little Girl*. The pastel cabin has soft gray lines, like the thick pencils from kindergarten. (Paper dolls have a hard time interacting with their environment.)

The dog in winter finds dead things: a rotten apple hard with ice, a dead squirrel curled back on itself like a snake. What does it mean to overwinter if you are microscopic: how to put up the summer's abundance, for the cold time? Turnips and carrots from the porch in Kalamazoo, each week a little more defeated: the cold pocked roots look chewed. What makes its winter home there?

Imagine the bustling interspecies town of a children's book. A population stable without bloody predation. Each animal has its special job. The skunk is a grocer. The cat, a mechanic, wears a dapper blue suit. Birds pick up litter in the park, the chipmunk teaches school, and the squirrel drives a truck. The animals, all small, fit on the bus together for a field trip to the farm. The mice that put out fires will never be dwarfed by the bear's burning house.

(Winter's sky is full of fractals. Dusk demands more of the heart. Keep driving although you should turn.)

PART II

HOW TO WRITE

A SUBURBAN MEMOIR

Lessons in disappointment

The baby was small and silent. She had soft yellow hairs. In the hospital they
brought her a hairbrush, special for babies. Waiting in the car on the way to see
her they took turns holding the hairbrush, rubbing its soft white bristles on their
sweaty palms. It was June. The baby came home. The two little animals helped
with everything. They gave her a bath in the sink. They picked her up off the bed.
One time, though, she slid to the floor and screamed. The one who dropped her
screamed too, screamed longer than the baby did. The mother shushed her and put
all three into the car, to take her to art class.

The art class was called *painting T-shirts*. It lasted a week and each day they painted
a different T-shirt. Then for the rest of the summer you could wear the T-shirts
that you painted and when school started again you could feel very special, in your
T-shirt, unless you had to wear a uniform. One day it was tie-dye. Another day
they used glitter to make fireworks. She tracked it into the car and through the
house. Flecks of glitter on the dinner table that night. The day the baby slid off the
bed it was dinosaurs. She was late because the baby slid off the bed so there was
only one dinosaur left, an ugly rhinoceros. There was only one shirt left. It was
mint green, a big man's shirt, with a pocket. The teacher attached the rhinoceros to
the ugly shirt for her. She sat on her tall stool and outlined the rhinoceros in gold
puff paint. It was cold in the art room and all the children worked quietly on their
T-shirts.

A list of things that happen

A door slammed. Miss Finch at school, innocent in her tank top, was embarrassing (*touch my arm*, she would say in a science lesson, *you can feel the condensation*). Made a cream cheese sandwich: soft white food you can eat while thinking about something else. Maybe the dog ran away. Maybe they were relieved that the father came home very, very late (even though it made their mother sad). Practiced cursive, the loops and swirls hard to make smooth.

(In *Little House in the Big Woods*, Pa makes bullets. They kill the pig. Laura and Mary play with its bladder like a kickball. Ma makes headcheese, which is not cheese. They put everything in the wagon when it's time to go.)

Notes for a suburban memoir

1.

I catalogued all her T-shirts in my head.

She stenciled shirts with the president's face on them to protest the brand new war.

She made me one. My mom said I couldn't wear it. (Something she'd made, against my skin.)

2.

She got mono and was out for two weeks. Felt empty after sixth period, almost heartbroken. Sometimes if I wasn't looking down at my shoes, or the speckled linoleum, or someone else's legs, she'd wave—once caught my arm, which tingled all through art class, like horror in a dream.

More notes for a suburban memoir

I grew up near a famous, once-sexy beach. Girls go wild in the bed of a pickup truck, the backseat of a convertible. (Spilling out the sides.) They patrol the edge of the sea at five miles per hour, grinding the sand down finer and finer. Honk and eat snow cones from the chair rental man. Their mouths rimmed sticky in the shimmering heat. Thick boys play Frisbee, jumping and rolling like busy dogs.

Try to avoid the sea turtle nests which are marked with orange plastic ribbon, like the edge of a construction zone: no trespassing. The leathery fists below the sand. Sometimes when they hatch they inch on their bellies, ribbed like the roof of a mouth, towards the bright hotels instead of the soft ocean edge.

When this happens, they die.

Some say, when light ordinances are proposed, that the sea turtles need to evolve faster. Survival of the fittest. Teach their nervous systems the difference between floodlights and the moon.

Notes to hold the place

Underage, we were refused entrance to the House of Leather. Instead, we lay in the Gay/Lesbian/New Age/Native American aisle of the local corporate bookstore, reading *Best Lesbian Erotica*.

Later, I bought the book with my babysitting money, hid it in my camera bag, a leathery gift from my dead grandfather, in the closet. As if to incubate. The book started to smell like wood and dust, like my grandfather's house. Each time I opened it, though, the stories were the same.

She had left for college. I would send her e-mails about the book. *People don't really do this, do they?* She wrote back telling me not to worry. She fell in love, she broke her arm. She would see me at Thanksgiving. (Signed with a sideways heart.)

For instance there was Troi the butch cop, who wore a pinky ring and cruised for straight women at clubs. She fucked them in the backseat of her black SUV, behind tinted windows. Each time I had a crush on Troi, until the penetration started. I would put the book back in the camera bag, in the closet. Shaking with something like disgust: a scabby girl, bewildered.

I couldn't figure out who these things happened to. Or how.

Failure to write a suburban memoir

Has anyone ever asked you to *pull yourself together*? Instead of *now I lay me down to sleep*, it's what parents in yellow houses whisper as they tuck their children into bed.

This is a song of praise and of mourning. I am writing this because I love the suburbs. This is the beautiful swell of music when she comes in the morning to take you to school (she is about to leave, and soon you will know how to drive yourself). The foggy morning, in her green car, and she slides onto the highway and you lean back and close your eyes, unafraid of dying. And then you are at school, and she puts her arm around your shoulder. At the end of the day, the shadows grow long on the black asphalt and in the spaces between the few remaining cars.

(Nothing ever happens.)

Writing that makes your mother sad

This is an investigation into the relationship between the book and the body. After I went away to college, my mother found the book in my bedroom and said to my sister: *gross*. (But how else to know how? Books are for learning.)

There were no stories in that book about holding hands. I tried to write one and failed. None about how it feels to have someone trace the contours of your ear while watching *But I'm a Cheerleader* under a sleeping bag, waiting tensely for her stepfather to come home from work. Or about going to a construction site to make out because it's surrounded by woods, for a little while longer.

I think it is perverse
to write a memoir

It is not a real bedroom. There is not a real door, but a screen which she's covered in tissue paper decoupage, a translucent membrane through which her little brother's Pokémon cartoons jump and glow.

This is the closest you've ever come to someone else's clutter. It points to the body that lives inside; you dizzy. She turns off the overhead lights and plugs in a strand of Christmas bulbs: stars, draped over the iron bed frame. Everything pretty came hand-me-down from her glamorous aunt, a hairdresser. On the desk are paintbrushes, notebooks, hair ribbons. The walls are a faint green, like bile. The Christmas lights throw tiny patches of light on the green wall, spots of red and blue and a brighter green. The television, balanced on a shaky bookshelf, plays a quiet documentary about sea turtles.

The photograph you took of her last week hangs on the wall with a thin stripe of silver duct tape. She's standing at a construction site in the back of her neighborhood. A place that used to be woods. Soon, it'll be houses, big, empty ones made of foamy stucco, not small, like hers, stuffed with wind chimes and bunk beds and baby brothers. In the photograph she crosses one arm over her chest and looks away. Her hair, now bright red, is rendered a black blur.

Architecture lessons

The house in progress was like a dead bug. *Exoskeleton*, one of the small mammals thinks with satisfaction. A big word. A big house.

It had no front, like a doll's house. Reach in to move the little people around. They have pipe cleaners for legs. A house is more than you think. This is secret knowledge. What if something went wrong, building the house. A hole or a lost finger. It would be there always. Later when they tape pictures on their walls—unicorns, Japanese goth-pop stars, surfing posters—they remember the words: *drywall*. *Stud*. There's empty space between the wall and itself.

Meanwhile

They moved out of the old house to the house by the grandmother. New people moved into their old house—a boy with white blonde hair who went to their school.

It was a borrowed house, for waiting. Where the two little animals slept on cots, in a loft. They could look down and see their parents in the kitchen below. The baby slept in the room full of boxes. There were no pictures on the walls. There were just enough dishes. There was another family on the side of the wall, who probably heard, for instance, *dammit*, followed by the mother's name. The little animals didn't dare look over the edge. They were not thrill seekers.

Back at the construction site

The swimming pool was a white cold cave. They'd crawl carefully down it in their school uniforms like somber explorers. Walked along the curve with careful canvas paws. A little puddle at what would be the deep part, from the rain. They floated bits of wasted wood. The game was: a lonely lady waiting for her husband to come back from sea.

It was a game they never got tired of. Nothing ever happened, but just standing in the empty swimming pool. That made it special. Also dangerous. The game went like this. He was on a whaling boat. He was gone a long time. Hush, little baby. *Papa will come home soon.*

At the Prince of Peace Catholic Church Oktoberfest carnival

Her father wins a stuffed monkey for her, although she'd wanted a goldfish. Those were too hard. You had to land a tiny ball in the tiny fishbowl. She swore every time it looks like it should have gone in, it bounded away instead.

Better luck next time, says the person running the game, a teenage boy (scary).

In another game, you pull rubber ducks out of a moving little river. The number on the bottom means a prize. She gets a duck numbered six and wins a glowing bracelet. It is dark and she gets cold and her father trades dollars for chances to play games and for rides on the giant slide.

He thinks she likes this but actually she is terrified. She goes on it every year at the fair with him: they climb the metal stairs—really just a ladder—and she tries not to look down because she can almost imagine falling. The threads in her knees get tight, her brain begins to wobble and the people below are so tiny: as tiny as the ping-pong ball her father couldn't get into the fishbowl. At the top she will sit in his lap, on a burlap sack and they will fly down the steep yellow curve. Her mother and baby sister at the bottom will take a picture. (She pretends this is fun.)

Landscaping

Near the end the men came and rolled out giant sheets of grass. Later the little animals would build shelters and shacks with the leftover boards, where the sod ended. A sandy, scrubby forest, just over the line.

In the waiting house

The den where the parents sleep is so small. The bed barely fits and when they get scared in the night and crawl alongside their mother the space between the bed and the wall is almost not there. Their father has to get into bed by crawling up the bed and get to the bathroom by crawling across the bed on his big brown knees. They think a room with no space around the bed—a bed-sized room—would be the safest place. Or sleeping in the bathtub.

They knew the rain because it came through the kitchen ceiling and they marked the cold by whether they could smell smoke coming from their grandmother's chimney on the other side of the cul-de-sac. It was never that cold but sometimes the sun was crisp and bright and they would put on their sweatshirts and their mother would stand at the door and watch them walk over. She wouldn't shut the door until the grandmother shut hers with the girls inside.

Sometimes the whole family would eat breakfast there: enormous dishes of frothy yellow eggs, bacon, grape or strawberry jelly in a little flowered dish, huge squares of waffles. It seemed like they were always waiting for those breakfasts to be over. The grandmother would insist nobody help her with the dishes and the children would go stand under the grapefruit tree in the courtyard and the grandmother would rattle the ice in her plastic tumbler and they would each give her a hug and walk around the cul-de-sac to the house that they lived in for a little while, and everybody would smell like cigarettes and bacon, even the baby.

Memory notes

Where do babies come from? She thinks she sounds cute, like a child from a movie. She wants her mother to laugh and say, *you're so silly, don't you know that already*, and with relief she would nod and walk away and they would never talk about it again. Instead the mother checks out a book from the library. The book is horrible. In the book is a woman in a blue dress and high heels. Her husband has a nice brown beard and a sweater. They sit on a couch at night. A moon shivers through the window. They look lovingly at one another. The special snuggle that moves sperm from the father's body into the mother's uterus is not satisfactorily explained.

For Halloween she is a flamingo. She has a pink tutu and pink tulle in her hair. She has round circles of bright blush on her face. A heavy plastic nose hangs around her neck, has a bad plastic smell. She peers through the window connecting her preschool classroom to where her sister is, in kindergarten. Before they eat their cupcakes they must change back into their play clothes. She doesn't feel it's right, all the children taking off their clothes in the same room. She looks again at the door.

The mother offers to read the book to her. *It's okay*, she says, *I already read it.* The mother looks hurt. *Do you have any questions?* No.

She watches her father shave. All mammals have hair. She will never shave her face, but her father rubs shaving cream on her cheeks anyway. His hands are big and brown and move slowly, the way they do when he strokes the dog's ears and she looks away because it seems private. He wears a towel around his waist. She wears one of his undershirts. It's clean, but it has the man smell. Like dark wiry hair on a hard brown chest. The armpits are yellow and crispy, like the burnt edges of a fried egg. She rolls the hardness between her fingers. Her father's face is loose but the rest of him is tight. Even after he shaves she can tell where the hairs grow from. He turns away to put his pants on, but she stays.

(Later she will learn her father remembers almost nothing. None of the births. In the pictures he's wearing green scrubs and a cap. The red creatures were lifted out. He grins, bewildered.)

More notes for a memoir

A cell without a membrane is not a cell, just as a house without walls or roof is not a house.

Diffusion: Nothing is happening. You are fifteen. You are writing in your notebook all the time. You are in love.

In passive transport, the cell does not expend energy to move molecules. Instead, molecules diffuse; they move unaided from an area of greater concentration to one of lesser concentration.

You come home from school and it's clear your mother has been crying. *You don't have to get married, you know.* But then she also says: *why are you trying to look like a boy?* You are worried. One sister might try to kill herself. The other could stop breathing, in her sleep. Your mother might run away. Your father might kill her: this is an old worry. A vestige, like a penguin's wing. Or a spleen, or a tailbone. The dog doesn't get enough exercise. There are clumps of paint and glue on the fruit-punch carpet.

Some of what makes us

As soon as a memory begins to draw a line around itself
(the blurred edges of the powder puff on the back of the toilet)

I begin to doubt myself, remembering the airless house with pink linoleum floors
we would leave smelling like a bar although she was careful always to bathe and
    powder us.

Her smells for instance: dusty medicine cabinet, ashy fireplace.
Twist the sensation to see will it return to its original shape, inject it with various
    elements
to see if it is metallic or non-metallic, positive or negatively charged, acid or base.

Like making soap: what's left over tells you what is needed, what is loved.
Once we melted down crayons in the microwave to make a candle,
brown and mottled, with a shoelace wick. Didn't we?

She fed us rubber chicken in the shape of hearts and stars.
The squeeze of translucent grease, cold sweet ketchup
white bread thick with butter from the dish that sat on the counter.

The ever-glowing ashtrays—teal ceramic, white dishes
the little cigarette shapes small notches that a tiny pinky could fit.
Plastic tumbler of cheap vodka with lipstick stain, sweating.

Artificially flavored candy colors like the juice that's called *drink*
which she used to buy for us. Once as a special treat
I got to pick out a lipstick for her at the dollar store.

She had two secret garden patios connected by a screened porch for smoking
receiving callers and having cocktails and *hors d'oeuvres:*
which meant cheese dip and stale Pringles.

She had the best accessories: plastic beads,
a fake leather pouch with pinching clasp for cigarettes and lipstick
sequined shirts with exotic animals, pink slippers on her tiny, knobbed feet.

We constructed a whole world our parents didn't know about
from the things we learned there.

Here's how it happened

It is like the beginning of time.

No. It is like something bony, opening: a sea star or chrysalis, but rather than cracking, the space between molecules—the fences, driveways, medians, retention ponds—are all growing outward from invisible centers. Imagine the suburbs expanding this way: suddenly a green prairie between yourself and your neighbor: a sea of uniform blades too stiff to walk on. Getting to the mailbox tires your little legs, the shopping center is as far as Laura Ingalls' general store where Pa takes the furs at the end of the winter: a big dead bundle.

The hallways grow, dwarfing the photographs of a past remembered clean, scrubbed, sepia-faded. The greens bleed into one another, splitting off: the mitosis of hue. And your bed is vast, a cotton prairie. Folds and empty space are dangerous. Elastic. Things you know begin to knock around painfully as the suburb around your heart and lungs inflates quietly, like sneakers in a dryer.

(What is the space around the heart? Too-big houses, the plastic and cardboard ones crammed on a hill. A place you can't call a neighborhood. It grows and grows until you are a tiny child who's just moved, and you scream *Mom, Mom I need you*, because everyone is so far and you look out the window and there is a huge bird, necky, long legs beyond the faraway swing set, almost to the retention pond where you've been told you must not go: there are snakes and alligators and little girls can drown.)

Can you write the suburban girl?

The body is, always, embarrassing. Nadine from your chemistry class says, *tell her you like her*. Nadine has kissed many people—this is the most important boundary you think—kissing or not. High school is full of people kissing—the boy with an orange bowl cut and thick silver earrings leans against your locker to kiss his shiny girlfriend; her legs glitter with fruity lotion, cucumber melon or kiwi strawberry, stumpy toenails bright blue or pink. Once, he held up a VHS of *William Shakespeare's Romeo + Juliet* and told you he was going to watch it with her that afternoon. *Do you think she'll like it? Romantic, right?*

Excuse me. How could anyone touch your surfaces? You are embarrassed just thinking about it, busy being embarrassed all the time.

You take Nadine's advice because she has kissed many people.

After lunch you tell her. The words bleed together, a throb in your belly. *I have a crush on you*, you say, *I like you very much*. She walks you to class with one arm around your waist. Her skinny wrist rests on the small of your back. You are practically dying. *I like you a lot too...but I'm about to graduate.*

This is an excuse—you knew there would be an excuse. You are relieved.

Thoughts of bodies fail

Something needs to happen so you decide to kiss Nadine. You can only think about this because she said it first. You talked about it all last weekend. On the phone. Your parents went out of town and left you with your aunt, who swelled pregnant and played Zelda. Nadine called and you talked for five hours. About what? Oh nothing. You lay on the floor of your room, on your belly, making intricate collages with too much rubber cement.

Nadine says *you're hot.*

You have rubber cement on the tips of your fingers which you rub off onto your jeans. It breaks off into little threads, like an eraser does, leaving your fingers still gummy. You can't wash it off. You just have to wait for the feeling to go away.

You go to her house while your mother and sister go to the fair.

You sit on her bed and she sits at the desk. You take her picture with the cardboard camera you keep in your backpack, thinking this needs to be documented. (You will keep it tacked to your wall for several years.) Red shirt. Brown pants. Dirty hair. A gap between her teeth. She has stern parents who are not home.

Later, you follow your mother through the grocery store, testing the memory. Each time you remember Nadine's face coming towards yours you feel a sick thrill, a falling in your stomach, behind your knees. To have a body is to be embarrassed.

PART III

POSITIVE REINFORCEMENT

FOR PETS AND OTHER

ANIMALS

No cats

The friend made it her business to disagree with everything. She was that kind of best friend.

Do you think Mr. Goodwin is creepy?
No, I like him. He's my swim coach.

Then they read her mother's *Cosmopolitan*. They wrote stories about sex. (*Hot ass. Thanks. Let's fuck.* They learned "let's fuck" from *Eyes Wide Shut*, which they were not supposed to watch.) They dared each other to hump Bob, which was the name they gave to her pillow: a synthetic fiber boyfriend. Grinding bony hips, slightly hysterical. They took off their shirts and wrote on each other's backs with ballpoint pens. To feel the metal drag over their untouched skin.

The next morning they climbed a huge pile of dirt in the neighborhood, where a house was going to be built. They invented boyfriends. One was a prince and the other was a knight. They looked up at the smoky gray sky and thought about love, its statistical impossibility. Books were better, and chat rooms.

Then Monday it was school again.

Mr. Goodwin swam in the 1968 Summer Olympics in Mexico City. 100 meter freestyle, butterfly, backstroke. Felt uneasy for days when he said, *you look mature with your hair down.* Strange little animal, leggy and quiet like an overgrown plant in that bland Episcopal uniform. Didn't wait to attract extra attention. Pulled her hair back tight, pressed her spine hard to walls.

Sometimes they had a special version of church called X-Treme Worship. All the middle schoolers would go to the Church Annex. It was a time to share feelings, if they had to do with God. Or peer pressure. They sang rock songs about salvation. Mrs. Breckenridge the Christian Education teacher was in charge. She liked to talk about babies in Africa, and why gay people get AIDS. When the little mammal complained to her mother, she said, *Mrs. Breckenridge is a Baptist, honey.* She imagined John the Baptist and was no less confused. Mrs. Breckenridge led them in faith-based metaphors: baby food jars full of sand, brightly colored ribbons to wear around their wrists, turning off the lights. One time at X-Treme Worship Mr. Goodwin whispered in her ear, *I want to read about you finding a cure for cancer one day.* It didn't even make any sense. She didn't want to be a scientist.

Miss, he would call her. Found reasons to speak soft and low in her ear, pinch dog hairs off her sweater in class. Picking at the evidence with hamburger hands: *Miss, do you have a cat?*

Once, we feared scurvy

The little mammals pack the wagon. They travel westward. *Chin up, girls!*

One slides a beach ball under her dress. She crosses the prairie with a baby tucked inside a narrow, hairless animal body. She does not invent a father for it.

Small creatures in long dresses and aprons. Bonnets from a trip they went on—to a place where people act like the olden days. A blacksmith, a weaver, and you could watch someone make candles. Everything is gray or brown in the past. A great-great-grandmother made the aprons. They never met her, so they don't have to be sad that she's dead.

They limit themselves to historical fiction. Flesh wounds. Nobody dies. Father is away in the war. He is a chaplain, never a soldier. He will come home, but not for many months. A messenger boy told them so.

They play quietly; they know this game will scare their mother.

Little mammals explore surfaces

A fine film coated all her surfaces. Cigarette ashes, gray dust from the fireplace, and makeup that she pressed into her wrinkles. What the little mammals' mother called blush, the grandmother called rouge.

She could feel herself leaving fingerprints, footprints wherever she went in the house. Like Hansel and Gretel she could tell where she came from. She crept into the bathroom. Opened the cabinet. All kinds of good things. Nail polish remover, pink like fruit punch. Piles of cotton balls and flat cotton circles that squeaked if you put them in your mouth.

A drawer of makeup. The bright rouge, blue and green eyeshadow. Foundation, which was also the name of the cement bottom of the new house. Soft thick pencils for outlining eyes and mouth. Everything felt silky and moist and smelled like crayons. Like touching moss in the woods, the green pompoms that grew near where the new house would be. When she shut the drawer her hands were a mix of all the colors—pink and brown like her skin was already, but with flakes of the other colors too. All the plastic windows were fogged over with makeup dirt.

The grandmother sat on the porch with Ron and smoked and drank. They were making bets. They were playing cards. Ron was the grandmother's boyfriend. They knew this even though nobody told them so. Ron was horrible. He looked like Santa Claus. Would you want to see Santa Claus on your grandmother's porch playing cribbage? No.

Ron went all over the world on airplanes. He loved China best. Sometimes he brought them presents—little tubes of gritty toothpaste labeled in another language. *What do you say, girls?*

Ron once had a Chinese wife. Then he didn't. Ron's son had a Chinese wife too. Ron also loved motorcycles and Indians. He wanted the little animals to sit on his lap while he told them stories about Indian maidens. Ron was pretending all the time. That's why they were scared of him.

There were ashtrays everywhere. Ashtrays in the bathroom. Next to the bed. In the kitchen. The kitchen smelled like bacon plus cigarettes. A fatty smell that stuck to them.

The grandmother smoked while she gave them a bath. With Mister Bubble. At home they couldn't because it gave them a rash on their privates. *Just a little.* The grandmother smiled with her big teeth they knew were fake. She put them in a glass in the bathroom after they fell asleep. *The rules are different here. You don't even have to tell Mom.* But they would, because at least one of them was obsessed with honesty.

Then it was time to get into bed and pretend to be asleep while she watched the news. The little animals nested under a beach towel, because the grandmother didn't have blankets. She didn't need them. Her skin was so big and she was always hot.

The news was better than a scary movie. It made a thrill in her pelvis, a jellyfish feeling: a sting, liquid, spreading. She rolled over with a fake murmur to see the TV out of slitted eyes. A man with a moustache explained about Mad Cow disease.

Sneaking is an important skill. You shouldn't do it all the time, but you should know how. She felt her hipbones to make sure they were still there. Her nightgown made static sparks under the dirty sheets.

More lessons in architecture

They watched the new house as it happened. First it was just trees, tall and thin. Their bark turned black when it rained. The mother told them it would take a whole year. While it got built they would keep living in the old house. Then when it took too long they lived in a borrowed house, on their grandmother's cul-de-sac.

Before it was a house, it was a stack of thin gray graph paper called plans. The mother and father sat at the dining room table and the little animals stood by them and the baby sat on the mother's lap and they all looked at the plans. *See, this will be your room.* One of the parents pointed to a blue box. The small animals nodded, confused.

They cut down some trees, but they left some, too. She was worried about the trees, but her mother said it was just a few. You can't make a place for the house without cutting down trees. Then it was a concrete slab. It was an architecture lesson. Each day stopping after school to see that day's progress. The word was *foundation*. Cool triangles of metal were called sometimes *brackets*. Then a wooden skeleton, golden planks with names like *two by four*. *Plywood*. Wood and metal had to hold the ceiling up, the roof on. It seemed impossible. The builders left a giant pile, some with nails in them still, that they used for years after, for projects.

Little animals in transit

The small mammal in the waiting house bristles her fur, dresses impatiently for school. Waiting for winter. The polyester jumper and monogrammed shirt. The blue sneakers. She is not the pretty one. The littler one puts on lipstick and a fancy dress. It is Picture Day. Some mammals do not like to have their pictures taken, but this one vows to be fancy.

Downstairs the air flips over, which is something they both can feel. It is normal. It happens frequently.

Downstairs the baby has been taken out of her room—the one full of all the boxes that wait until they go to the new house. The mother makes coffee. Takes sugar out of the cabinet. Stirs in powder (pretend milk).

The father calls up the stairs that he's leaving for work. *Bye Daddy*, they call, in their best little girl voices.

No time for empathy

I would like you to be normal now, one little mammal thinks to the other at breakfast. Breakfast is something called Carnation Instant Breakfast, which is like baby formula for children who do not want to eat breakfast. Or it is a banana. Those are the options. The other little mammal, the smaller one, will not put on her shoes. She is crying. *I hate socks*, she says. *They feel horrible.*

It is a time for quickness. The mother grabs a little foot. Wrestles it into a sock, pink with white lace. The little animal is also pink, with white lace. Her tears make her wet so she looks like a newborn puppy.

(A certain book from the school library shows puppies being born. Out of the mother dog's vagina. They all crowd around it at free choice library time. When it's time to go back to the classroom the next student on the list gets to take the book home for a whole week.)

Small mammal's worldview, circa 1991

The small mammal stands on a kitchen chair. The mother explains about the Berlin Wall. She is shaping a meatloaf. *There were people on each side and they couldn't get through to the other side because different people owned the different sides.*

Her hands are sticky and brown, the wedding band gluey. Her perfect oval fingernails usually taste like cigarettes and hand lotion. Now they have meat under them. The little animal wants to help, but she is scared to touch the meat. It makes a zipper sound as the mother pats it. *Sometimes people tried to climb over to see their families, and they got shot and died.*

She is scared of her teeth falling out. The mother has to wiggle them. Otherwise she will have too many teeth, the big teeth and the baby teeth in her mouth together. They will stick straight out and cram into each other. She will look like a bad creature, a biting creature. The dentist will have to put her to sleep and take some out. (The veterinarian put her dog to sleep last year.)

Next, they make brownies from a box. That winter the grandmother broke her leg in the laundry room, on moving day. Little mammal bones freeze when old ladies fall down. Like a museum skeleton. *Did you push her?* The almost-grown uncle, sunburned, joked. Little mammal horror is a wide-eyed sadness, like needles.

There was a war on TV. A raging sandstorm and a voiceover. She wanted to watch something colorful. Nested in flowered sheets worn warm, so tiny, she felt guilty even asking. She put the covers over her head and slithered between the parents' animal legs. A dry brown leg, with a man smell, like shirts from the hamper. Dry brown leg; soft white leg, with blue veins. The mother covers up the blue veins with skirts, even when she goes swimming. Little animals like to touch people's skin.

But they knocked the wall down, the mother said. The small mammal felt relieved but was not sure why. Digging her fingers into the batter. Looking for chocolate chunks.

The little animal slept in a room with a big glass door. Anything big and glass was not safe. Little animals know this. The door let out to bushes, the green front yard and eventually the street. She knew how to turn two corners and get to the park.

At the park people put their boats in the gray river. Sometimes you could see manatees: underwater elephants with a scar where the trunk should be. Sometimes the boats went too fast and hit the manatees. They had to Adopt-A-Manatee at school. They put nickels into a jar for the manatee and her picture hung on the wall. Teenage boys lurked at the park. The slide was too tall, and metal. It would burn you in the summer. Their father called it *a lawsuit waiting to happen* and then he made them go home. The park made the mother nervous.

The whole world watched on TV and now people can move freely.
Sometimes she fell asleep listening to the war and it got in her dreams.

Natural selection produces
a colorful world

He buried a bone Monday. Like a dog in a movie. When we walk past that spot now he gets smug, wags faster. He knows better than to trust the kibble supply. He will be the perfect survivalist patriot when the collapse comes. He has gallon jugs of water and canned food in the basement. Buries open-pollinated seeds in waterproof containers, deep in the woods. Maybe I should do these things, but I am too domesticated.

Under domestication, the uniformity of the wild form is replaced by extreme variability, especially in color.

Domestication is the conversion of wild things into things that sleep in the bed. Things that bark in the night and don't know why. He is a child with nightmares, my own small self. Nobody made me sleep alone when I was scared. He hears coyotes, and other things I cannot.

The wild has no reason to lie across the lap, to hold a hand between jaws playfully. Self-control and soft teeth. It is kibbles to be eaten, forget the warm squirming things. (Now, a pet can be vegan.)

Domestication lessons

Ben asks why we're taking the eggs. *If she sits on it, won't it make another duck?*
In his worldview, more ducks are only ever a good thing. His eyes are wide and
sideways, like a goat. He's wearing two different shoes: one that ties and one with
Velcro.

*If there was a male duck, a drake, he would fertilize the eggs. But since we don't have
a boy duck they'll only just stay eggs.* He crouches in the shitty straw to talk to the
ducks and the chickens. *Then why do they lay eggs*, he asks, *if they're not going to
become babies.*

What does he imagine when I say "fertilize"?

2. BEN, ON RATS

Everybody thinks they're vicious but really it's just because they are prey for so many other animals. He lists some off on his fingers: *people, owls, cats. Rats are very smart. They just have to work so hard to find food and shelter, and to raise their babies, and that's why they get mean sometimes.*

I have a friend who works in like a science place and every day for two hours she gets to play with the rats. They climb up her arms and sit on her head. To keep them busy when they're not doing experiments.

3. HOW BEN GOT HIS RATS

The first because he asked for a gerbil, and they learned rats are smarter and live longer. The second because they saw a sweet little rat about to be eaten by a snake at the pet store in Grand Rapids. *One of my rats died from lymphoma, do you know what that is?* Another rat was a consolation, after his dog died. *We were all really sad, but actually now I'm sort of glad because I got Lucy.*

4. BEN, ON SNAKES

One of Ben's rats he saved from a caged snake, bored and hungry. He knows his beloveds are prey.

You can't ever give snakes gerbils, he says, *they're like ice cream. If you feed a gerbil to a snake they won't ever eat rats again. Gerbils are too good.*

Night Step

She asks has he done the Ninth Step with me, but I mishear
my imagination delineates something more perfect
more elegant than all the world's scripted apologies.

I hold his arm or he holds mine (it doesn't matter which)
we step over the threshold into a summer night
mosquitoes and stars, the wind in the trees, all that.

We would chew wintergreen Lifesavers
make sparks between our teeth
like static electricity.

I would tell him why pirates wore eyepatches:
so one eye could see in the dark,
always ready to go below.

We would know the words to put to the bird calls
hear the cicadas' seven year hum
gesture with whispers to the things we could not see.

He would point to the North Star
and teach me to calculate latitude
based on the angle of geography to the sympathetic nervous system.

We would walk alone for a moment and choose new names
unbounded by signifiers of *father* and *daughter*
crazy and *afraid of being crazy.*

Intervention

A baby bird the first time opening his mouth to me, all wide red and hollow, too delicate to be living, perfect like a museum display varnished and under glass, stuck with pins and paper tags: *trachea, esophagus, crop.*

We saw him outside the barn. My mother, on the phone when I told her later: *you go get that baby bird.*

He tips back to take the soggy dog biscuit and trembles. Full, stony eyelids pinch shut the prehistoric face and then he nests with tube sock and twigs.

My mother as a teenager had a boyfriend who stole baby birds for her. Squirrels, too, from the trees ringing his uncle's golf course. She fed them dog food out of a can and also made soft nests.

The animal question, again

One kindergartener wrote on his All About Me poster: *I can scratch animals on their chin.*

Maybe there is something wrong that it just occurred to me: to wonder about what you're thinking as our bodies move solid and soft together, as you push aside my wool, flannel and cotton around my ankles. I think instead sometimes of evolution: cell division, the natural selections, other coital interminglings. Conjugal seconds and hours; millions of years' nuclear fission. Cells splitting into new coiled strands, long but decipherable, thick with magic, like the seed catalog we pore over all winter.

I like to think in mythical terms of our animal sex, evolution mated to imagination: hybrid vigor, sterile offspring. We debate what bodies want, and how is that instinct: how we inscribe desires onto the bodies we have, describe: furry, uncertain.

Mammals hold each other at times like this, licking fur and eyelids. When we wake to the radio, when I rub the side of your thigh at a party, I ask myself (ask you, ask all of us) what does it mean to be a mammal—who will scratch us on the chin?

Notes

Much of this work owes an imaginative debt to Laura Ingalls Wilder's *Little House* series. For an excellent critical and historical discussion of Wilder's work (including the racism that the books are rightfully criticized for) I suggest reading "No-Man's-Land" in *Notes from No Man's Land* by Eula Biss or *The Wilder Life* by Wendy McClure.

The light, persistent touch of Donna Haraway's *The Companion Species Manifesto* and *When Species Meet* might be felt throughout.

Other vital texts include E.B. White's *Charlotte's Web*, Emily Dickinson's Poem 254, Tristan Taormino's *Best Lesbian Erotica 2003*, *The Busy Busy World* and other picture books by Richard Scarry, and various homesteading and animal husbandry guides (especially *The Country Living Encyclopedia* by Carla Emery, Dirk van Loon's *The Family Cow*, and *Storey's Guide to Raising Dairy Goats* by Jerry Belanger).

"The Miracle of Life at the Chelsea Community Fair" excerpts text from *Thank Goodness for Cows*, a coloring book produced by the National Dairy Council. In "More notes for a memoir," the italicized description of diffusion came from *Smithsonian Science 101: Biology* by George Ochoa.

Acknowledgements

I am so grateful for Sawako Nakayasu, who left a comment on my blog that said she wanted to publish my book—which she proceeded to do warmly, thoughtfully, and with great speed—all of which were felt and appreciated across the vast distance that separates us.

Many thanks to the editors who published earlier versions of the following pieces: "Sav-a-kid," "At the Allegan County Fair," "Shorthand," and "Anatomy lessons" appeared in *3:AM Magazine* in July 2011. *Specter* first published "An education in electricity and green things" in December 2011. "The animal question," in slightly different form, was published in *Glitter Tongue* (February 2012).

So much tenderness and gratitude for my mentors at Goddard, with whom I wrote and incubated *Domestication Handbook:* Douglas A. Martin, Rebecca Brown, Elena Georgiou, and in particular Bhanu Kapil, who saved me. Thank you for holding the space for writing and for the wild unicorn pack, for taking this girl between your jaws, for sprinkling me with sweet oils when I wretched and quivered. "Are you shaking?" Bhanu asked. Yes.

A low residency program means not being bound to one community while one is in school, and my book and my subjectivity are indebted to the strange and magical places I lived while working on earlier drafts of this book: Richard Andres and Deb Lentz, whose Tantré Farm was a frightening and joyful introduction to farming; Cathy and Tom Halinski's sweet LaMancha goats, their wild orchard, and their impeccable milking parlor, where I watched death for the first time; the summer camp and community at Circle Pines Center, where Rachel, Kevin, Kat, and Tom listened to me read my poetry in the farmhouse library.

Writings on queerness and the girl were instrumental to my revision process, and for that I have immense gratitude for my tumblr friends, the wallpaper corner, the cutting edge, of theory.

So much thanks to Kristen Nelson, for her generous edits in purple scrawl. To Dess, who painted my nails the weekend I started to feel like a real writer (AWP 2012). To Ariel for her love that crosses back and forth across this country. My theory friends (Marielle and Nic, especially). To the unicorn pack and the rest of the Goddard community for the things you do with language. To my friends in Gainesville and all over, who are all supportive and sustaining in so many ways.

Most especially to my family, who I love in ways a text can only grossly approximate: my mother and my sisters, my father, the extended web of others, animals, and ghosts: even/especially when it is difficult. This book is for you.

To Jasmine: velveteen rabbit, swamp lover, sweetest reader, my heart. Thank you.

The author

KRISTEN STONE has had work published in *Glitter Tongue, Women's Studies Quarterly, 3:AM*, and elsewhere. She is a poetry editor for *Limn Literary & Arts Journal* and runs Unthinkable Creatures, a chapbook press, out of her home. Kristen lives in Gainesville, Florida where she works as a youth advocate. This is her first book.

Photograph by Lisa Stone

CPSIA information can be obtained at www.ICGtesting.com
Printed in the USA
BVOW022339020712

294200BV00002B/1/P